Izzy and Frank

written by
Katrina Lehman

illustrated by
Sophie Beer

To my beautiful sisters, Mills and Sah—
For a childhood of wildness and unconditional love and for adventures
still to be shared.
　　　　　—Treen

To dearest Charlotte Rose,
We grew up on beaches; you grew up to be the funniest, sparkliest
person I know.
　　　　　—Sophie

The illustrations in this book were made with a combination
of traditional mark making and digital medium.

Typeset in Futura by the publisher.

Scribble, an imprint of Scribe Publications
18–20 Edward Street, Brunswick, Victoria 3056, Australia
2 John Street, Clerkenwell, London, WC1N 2ES, United Kingdom
3754 Pleasant Ave, Suite 100, Minneapolis, Minnesota 55409 USA

First published by Scribble 2020

This book is printed with vegetable-soy based inks, on FSC® and other controlled certified paper from
responsibly managed forests, ensuring that the supply chain from forest to end-user is chain of custody
certified. Printed and bound in China by 1010.

9781925849509 (Australian hardback)
9781912854684 (UK hardback)
9781950354238 (North American hardback)

Catalogue records for this title are available from the
National Library of Australia and the British Library

scribblekidsbooks.com

FSC
www.fsc.org
MIX
Paper from
responsible sources
FSC® C016973

Izzy loved her island.
Her house had no corners and
a staircase that twirled high into the sky.
From her bedroom, she spied
dolphins diving and stingrays gliding.

She loved the wind that
whistled and wailed and
the waves that lapped at her feet.

But most of all, she loved Frank.

Every morning, Izzy woke to find Frank waiting patiently.

After breakfast, they set off around their island with buckets and sandwiches.

For Sale

Although Frank usually couldn't wait until lunch.

On grey-storm-rainy days, they dug up
treasure, played hide-and-seek
and drew pictures in the sand.

On blue-sky-sunny days,
they swam with seals,
hunted crusty crabs and
poked sparkly, spiky starfish.

On wild-wind-blowy days, they outraced sea monsters,

and fought off pirates.

And some days things just happened
when all they were doing was counting sand.

Every night, after the sun sank into the sea,

Frank and Izzy fell asleep to the sounds of their island.

But one morning, everything changed.

Izzy hated the city. Her new house was small, with sharp corners. There were no winding stairs and no views of the sea.

The streets were narrow and busy,
and traffic hummed late into the night.

She didn't understand the other children
and the games they played.

She was told to 'Wear shoes' and
'Sit still' and 'Be quiet, please'.

Izzy ached for the wind in her hair and the taste of sand and salt in her mouth.
She missed her lighthouse. She missed her island.

And most of all, she missed Frank.

Every day and every night, Izzy searched
the grey streets and the grey sky.
But Frank didn't come.

Then, one morning, Izzy woke to something tugging on her hair.

And there was Frank, waiting patiently.

After breakfast, the two of them set out with sandwiches to explore her new home.

They buried treasure,

WHARF MARKETS

played hide-and-seek,

and drew pictures on the walls.

They swam in the fountain,
chased butterflies in the park
and fought off pirates.

And at the end of the day,
they ate chips and fell asleep
to the sounds of her new home.

Now, every morning,
Izzy wakes to the sound
of the sea and the city.

She knows she will
never forget her island…

...and that Frank will be
with her wherever she goes.

HMS Frank